Fair of Hearts

Ulrich Germania

Imprint

Book title:
Fair of Hearts

Subtitle:
Short, kitschy fairground story

Series:
Romantic Encounters at the Funfair

AI Note:
AI generated story, initiated and revised by the author
Translated from German into American English by an AI.

Author:
Ulrich Germania © 2025

Publisher:
BoD · Books on Demand GmbH, In de Tarpen 42,
22848 Norderstedt, bod@bod.de

Print:
Libri Plureos GmbH,
Friedensallee 273, 22763 Hamburg

ISBN: 978-3-7693-8867-1

Table of contents

Picture credits:

The images on the book cover and the illustrations in the book were generated by AI and modified using programs for photo manipulation.

AI Note:

Author Ulrich Germania came up with the characters and the plot, the AI wrote the story, then it was revised and improved. The translation from German into American English was also done by an AI.
The translation was checked and approved.

The Funfair

The lights of the amusement park shone into the night, transforming the fairground into a sea of colors. Bright strings of lamps stretched like glowing garlands between the rides, while the music from the carousels and attractions filled the air with a mixture of pop music and excited voices.

People were crowded everywhere - families with children, groups of young people and couples of all ages. They had all come to escape everyday life for a few hours and immerse themselves in the magical world of the funfair.

The Ferris wheel spun majestically at the edge of the square, offering passengers a breathtaking view of the glittering scenery. Next to it, a chain carousel whirled its passengers through the air, accompanied by enthusiastic screams.

The bumper cars, surrounded by flashing neon lights, were a magnet for young people who chased each other in the colorful cars.

Stalls lined up between the rides: shooting galleries lured visitors with plush prizes and lottery booths promised great fortune.

The aroma of roasted almonds, fresh popcorn and spicy sausages drifted enticingly across the grounds, as chips sizzled in oil and schnitzel sizzled on the grill at the food stalls. The sweet smell of candy floss mingled with the tangy aroma of beer from the festival's beer gardens.

The atmosphere was electrifying. Laughter and music blended into a joyful crescendo as visitors moved from one attraction to the next. Every corner of the fair promised a new adventure, a new chance for fun and excitement.

As the night progressed, the fair only seemed to come alive. The lights shone brighter, the music grew louder, and the energy of the crowd pulsed like a living heartbeat through the alleyways between the attractions.

It was a world of its own, an oasis of joy and light-heartedness that captivated every visitor and promised the magic of timeless pleasure.

Lisa and Anna

On this balmy Saturday evening, Lisa and Anna were sitting in their shared apartment in the city center.

Lisa, a 25-year-old graphic designer with long blonde hair and a penchant for fancy earrings, was bored and flicking through a magazine. Anna, a 24-year-old nurse, was lying on the sofa scrolling through her smartphone.

"I don't want to watch Netflix again this Saturday," Lisa moaned and threw the magazine aside. "We have to do something!"

Anna looked up from her cell phone. "Yes, I'm bored too. Do you have any better ideas than going to the usual bars?"

At that moment, Lisa's cell phone vibrated. She opened the message, and her eyes lit up.

"Anna, that's it! The events calendar I subscribe to says that the funfair is in town today. Let's go to the funfair!"

Anna sat up with interest.

"Funfair? That sounds like fun! I haven't been to a fair like that for ages."

"Exactly!" exclaimed Lisa enthusiastically. "Candy floss, bumper cars, maybe even a ride on the Ferris wheel. That would be something different."

The two friends jumped up and started to get ready. Lisa chose her favorite short jeans and a crop top, and Anna said, "Good idea, I'll dress like that too."

"Don't you think that's too sexy?" asked Anna as the girls looked at themselves in the large mirror.

"Who knows," Lisa said with a mischievous smile as she combed her hair, "maybe we'll meet some nice guys."

Anna laughed. "At the funfair? That would be like a cheesy romance novel."

"Sometimes life writes the best stories," Lisa replied and winked at her friend.

The two friends set off with excited anticipation. The streetcar stopped right in front of the fairground. When they got off, they immediately heard the music, saw lots of people and the smell of popcorn and the colorful lights immediately got them in the mood.

Lisa and Anna were ready for an evening of adventure and who knows - maybe even a surprise that would change their lives.

Marcus and Lukas

This Saturday evening, Marcus and Lukas were sitting in Marcus' apartment. The 28-year-old architect was lounging on the sofa while his best friend Lukas, 27, an electrical engineer, opened a bottle of beer.

"Dude, what are we doing today?" asked Lukas and took a big gulp.

Marcus shrugged his shoulders. "I don't know. Back to the student quarter with all the pubs and students?"

At that moment, Lukas' cell phone flashed. It was a message from the event calendar he had subscribed to: "The summer funfair starts today at the fairground!"

"Marcus, let's go to the funfair!" shouted Lukas enthusiastically. "I'm sure we'll see some pretty girls there."

Marcus' eyebrow went up. "Funfair? How old school."

"Going to the pub is also old school! A funfair is just the thing," countered Lukas. "Bumper cars, Ferris wheel, great atmosphere. That's where you meet women!"

After a brief hesitation, Marcus agreed.

"It's summer. Jeans and a T-shirt, that's all you need to wear. We can actually start right away."

Marcus quickly put some gel in his hair, while Lukas put on his modern sneakers and waited at the door.

The anticipation grew. The two friends were ready for a funfair adventure - unsuspecting that this evening would be better than usual.

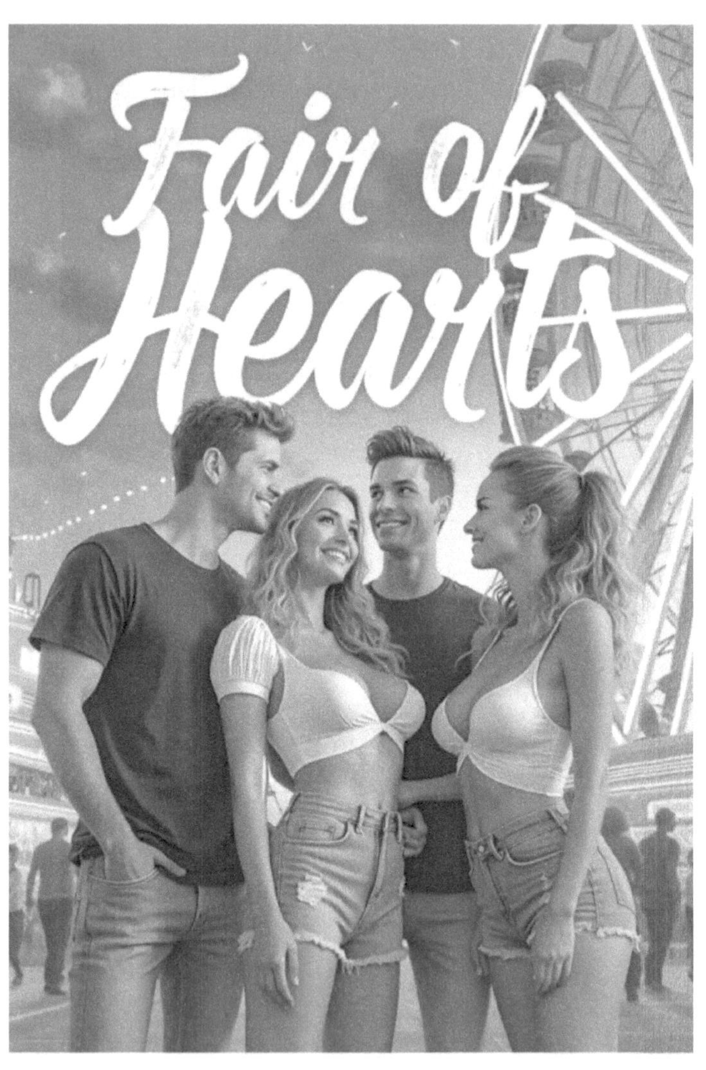
Fair of
Hearts

Encounter at the bumper cars

The funfair was buzzing with energy. Colorful lights flashed, music blared, and the bumper cars were the absolute hotspot for flirting and action.

Marcus and Lukas had just bought tokens when Lukas saw two girls.

"Dude, there are two sexy girls over there," he whispered, nodding his head towards Lisa and Anna, who were just taking a seat in a bumper car.

The girls got their electric car into position and waited for it to start. Lisa, with her skimpy top, sat at the wheel and stared unerringly at the young men who were just getting into a car. Anna noticed, laughed and winked at her friend.

"The hunt begins," shouted Marcus.

The first collision was intentional - Marcus deliberately rammed into the girls' car.

"So, you want to play!" Lisa shouted and laughed out loud.

Lisa countered immediately. made a perfect U-turn and thundered back. Lukas waved to Anna, who waved back, while Lisa and Marcus had to concentrate on driving.

A wild chase started. The cars chased back and forth, bumped into each other, swerved. Screaming girls, loud music, flashing lights - the perfect soundtrack for this moment.

After the short ride, everyone was out of breath with laughter. They felt the adrenaline and the pure joy of life.

As they got out of the cars, the boys approached the girls and Marcus just asked:

"Fancy an ice cream?"

"Sure!" Lisa and Anna replied at the same time.

The flirtation had begun.

Ice cream and first talks

The four of them strolled to an ice cream stand, still high on bumper car adrenaline.

"I'm Marcus," he said, grinning at Lisa. "And this is my buddy Lukas."

"Lisa," she replied with sparkling eyes and introduced her friend: "And this is Anna."

They ordered ice cream. Lisa chose strawberry flavor, Marcus chocolate, Anna vanilla and Lukas dared to try watermelon with mint.

"Great driving skills," praised Lukas and nudged Anna.

"You weren't bad either," she countered with a laugh.

They found a bench with a view of the Ferris wheel. The conversation flowed easily.

"What do you do?" asked Marcus.

Lisa talked about her job as a graphic designer and Anna said: "I hope you never see me at work. I'm a nurse and I don't want to see you sick in hospital."

Marcus laughed and said: "I'm an architect and I always wear a hard hat when I visit a construction site," and Lukas added: "I'm an electrical engineer and I always keep a safe distance from power lines."

"Sexy top," Marcus said to Lisa.

"Thank you, I designed it myself," she replied proudly.

The chemistry was right. Glances became more intense, people moved closer together.

"So, what's next?" asked Lukas with a grin.

The night was still young, and no one wanted it to end.

Joint tour of the fair

The rollercoaster towered high above the fairground. Marcus and Lisa, Lukas and Anna got on together. The carriages were cramped, the seats narrow.

"Ready?" asked Marcus, looking into Lisa's blue eyes with a grin.

She grabbed his hand. The first bend came - and pressed them closer together. Centrifugal forces did the rest. Lisa leaned against Marcus, Anna snuggled up to Lukas.

The train raced through loops and bends. Screaming, laughing, hearts pounding. The closeness and tension between the couples grew with every bend.

When they got out, their hands were still intertwined. The fair pulsated around them - music, lights, temptations.

"Where to next?" asked Lukas.

The night was young, the possibilities endless.

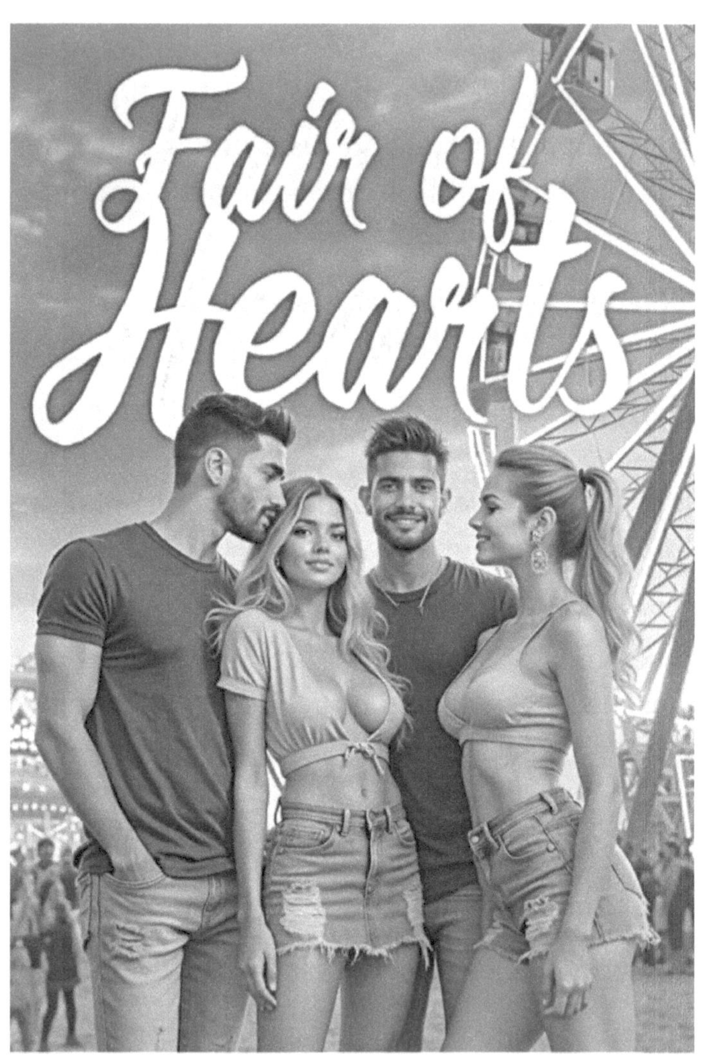

Fair of
Hearts

At the shooting range

A shooting range beckoned with colorful prizes and flashing lights. Marcus and Lukas exchanged meaningful glances.

"Ladies, allow us to demonstrate how to aim properly," Lukas boasted with a twinkle in his eye.

Lisa and Anna giggled with amusement.

"Let's see what you've got, boys!"

Marcus reached for the air rifle. Concentrating, he took aim at the target. Bang! Hit!

It was Lukas' turn. With his tongue between his teeth, he took careful aim. Bang! Also hit!

The stall owner grinned.

"Respect, boys! Choose your prizes!"

Without hesitation, they both pointed to the red roses.

"For you," Marcus said gently and handed Lisa the rose. Their fingers touched and a tingling sensation ran through her.

Lukas did the same and gallantly handed Anna the flower. "A rose for a rose," he whispered.

The girls blushed, their eyes sparkling in the light of the fairground lights.

"Thank you," Lisa breathed as she brought the rose to her nose. The sweet scent mingled with the smell of cotton candy and excitement.

The tension between them was almost palpable. The evening had become so romantic and neither of them wanted it to end.

Romance on the Ferris wheel

The funfair had transformed the night into a sea of lights. The gondolas of the Ferris wheel hovered majestically over the fairground, its colorful lights flashing auspiciously.

"Ready to fly high?" asked Marcus with a wink.

Lisa nodded, her heart beating faster.

They got into a gondola, Marcus and Lisa into one, Lukas and Anna into the next. Slowly, the wheel began to turn and they left the ground behind them.

"I'm a bit scared of heights," Lisa confessed quietly.

Marcus gently took her hand.

"Don't worry, I'm here."

With every meter they saw more of the nocturnal beauty of their city. A river glistened in the distance, the lights of the city spread out beneath them like a sparkling carpet.

Once at the top, the gondola stopped. The moment seemed to freeze.

"Lisa," whispered Marcus. She turned to him, her eyes gleaming in the glow of the lights.

Slowly, almost in slow motion, their faces approached. Lisa's heart raced when their lips finally met. The kiss was tender, full of promise.

In the neighboring gondola, Lukas and Anna experienced their own magical moment. Lukas and Anna sat closely together in their gondola.

Tension crackled in the air. Lukas turned to Anna and their eyes met. Slowly, their lips drew closer.

The first kiss was gentle, tender. The world around them blurred, only this moment mattered.

When the wheel started moving again, the couples were in each other's arms. The city spun beneath them, but for the lovers, the world stood still.

When they reached the bottom, they got out, holding hands. The couples approached each other, all with a knowing smile.

"So, how was it up there?" asked Lukas with a grin.

"Stunning," Marcus replied without taking his eyes off Lisa.

The fair continued to pulsate around them, but a new, exciting chapter had just begun for the four young people.

Dance and passion

The night was still young when Marcus and Lisa, Lukas and Anna discovered a beer garden hidden between trees and a wooden fence on the edge of the funfair. Colorful fairy lights stretched across the dance floor, disco hits from the 80s filled the air.

"Dancing?" Marcus asked the group and everyone was in favor.

The music of hits such as "Billie Jean" and "Girls Just Want to Have Fun" pumped through the speakers. The dance floor was full of people. Marcus pulled Lisa towards him, their bodies moving perfectly to the rhythm. Lukas and Anna danced next to them, looking deep into each other's eyes.

After a few drinks, the atmosphere became more exuberant. The couples kissed between the dance breaks, the funfair around them blurred.

"I can't believe we met by chance tonight," Lisa whispered in Marcus' ear.

He smiled: "Sometimes fate writes the best stories."

The night was full of promise, passion and unexpected moments.

Farewell and promise

The disco party at the fair was still pulsating when the operators began to close the stalls.

Marcus, Lisa, Lukas and Anna knew that the magical evening was coming to an end.

"We absolutely have to see each other again," Marcus said to Lisa.

They exchanged phone numbers and immediately set up a WhatsApp group called "Kirmes". This way, everyone knew the phone numbers of the other members and it was ensured that they could stay in touch.

The boys accompanied the girls to the exit of the funfair. Outside, Anna called a cab. While they waited, the couples made the most of the last few moments. Hot, passionate kisses merged under the colorful lights of the almost empty fairground.

The cab arrived. The newly in love couples parted with a promise to meet again, but only for a few hours.

When Lisa and Anna arrived home, they couldn't stop raving about the men they had met.

Lisa took the cell phone and wrote to the funfair group:

"Another fair visit tomorrow?"

"Yes!" everyone replied almost simultaneously.

The messages flew back and forth, full of anticipation for the next evening.

The night was over, the love story of the two couples had only just begun.

More Books by the Author

If you enjoyed this romantic, kitschy fairground story, then you are sure to enjoy other short stories that Ulrich Germania has come up with.

Many stories by the author tell of romantic encounters in unusual places.

AI-Note: For the following stories applies: Ulrich Germania came up with the characters and the plot, the AI wrote the story, and then the author revised and improved it.

Fair of Hearts
Short, kitschy fairground story
(this book)

Doctors at the funfair
Not a doctor's story, but somehow.

The Goddess of Love at the Fair
A fair with a mystical flair

In Love with Costumes
Romantic encounters at a cosplay event

Doctor's at the Funfair
Ulrich Germania

The Goddess of Love at the Funfair
Ulrich Germania